Eleanor
the Snow White
Fairy

To Erin, from the fairies

Special thanks to Rachel Elliot

Text copyright © 2016 by Rainbow Magic Limited

All rights reserved. Published by Scholastic Inc., 557 Broadway, New York, NY 10012, *Publishers since 1920*. SCHOLASTIC and associated logos are trademarks and/or registered trademarks of Scholastic Inc. Published by arrangement with Rainbow Magic Limited. Series created by Rainbow Magic Limited. RAINBOW MAGIC is a trademark of Rainbow Magic Limited. Reg. U.S. Patent & Trademark Office and other countries. HIT and the HIT logo are trademarks of HIT Entertainment Limited.

ISBN 978-0-545-85190-9

10 9 8 7 6 5 4 3 2 1   16 17 18 19 20

Printed in the U.S.A.   40

First edition, January 2016

Eleanor the Snow White Fairy

by Daisy Meadows

SCHOLASTIC INC.

The Fairyland Palace

Fairy Tale Lane

Rachel's House

Tippington Town

Jack Frost's
Ice Castle

Forest

Tiptop Castle

The Fairy Tale Fairies are in for a shock!
Cinderella won't run at the strike of the clock.
No one can stop me—I've plotted and planned,
And I'll be the fairest one in all of the land.

It will take someone handsome and witty and clever
To stop storybook endings forever and ever.
But to see fairies suffer great trouble and strife,
Will make me live happily all of my life!

Contents

A Surprise Reflection

When Kirsty Tate opened her eyes, for a moment she couldn't remember where she was. She gazed up at the canopy that hung over her four-poster bed. A spring breeze had pushed open the gauzy curtains, and the sun lit up the white dressing table with its gold and silver swirls. On the dressing table lay a book with a sparkling cover—*The Fairies' Book of Fairy Tales.*

A smile spread across Kirsty's face as she remembered everything that had happened the day before. She sat up and looked across to where her best friend, Rachel Walker, was still fast asleep.

"Rachel, wake up," she said in a gentle voice. "It's our second day at Tiptop Castle!"

Rachel opened her eyes and gave Kirsty a sleepy smile. They were staying in a beautiful old castle on the outskirts of Tippington, where the Fairy Tale Festival was being held. Their bedroom was at the top of a tower of the castle, and the girls had agreed that it was fit for a princess—or two!

"What are you going to wear today?" asked Kirsty, hopping out of bed and opening the big wardrobe where they had hung their clothes.

"How about our fairy dresses?" suggested Rachel, swinging her legs out of bed. "It will be fun to join in with everyone else."

The day before, all the festival organizers had been wearing fairy tale costumes. Kirsty clapped her hands together.

"That's a great idea," she said, "especially after our Fairyland visit yesterday!"

As they pulled on their beautiful fairy dresses, they talked about the adventure they had shared with Julia the Sleeping Beauty Fairy.

After they had met Hannah the Happily Ever After Fairy in the reading room of the castle, she had whisked them to Fairyland and introduced them to the Fairy Tale Fairies. The seven fairies had presented them with the beautiful *The Fairies' Book of Fairy Tales*.

When Kirsty and Rachel opened the book, the pages were blank. Jack Frost had stolen the fairies' magic objects, and now he had the power to rewrite the fairy tales to be about him and the goblins. The fairy tale characters had fallen out of their stories and were lost in the human world, along with the magic objects.

"I'm so happy that we managed to help Julia the Sleeping Beauty Fairy get her magic jewelry box back," said Rachel.

"And Sleeping Beauty and her prince are back in their story," Kirsty added. "But we have to do the same for the other fairies. They need their objects to look after their fairy tales."

She smiled as Rachel pulled on her

mini backpack with its glittery fairy wings. It was funny to wear fake wings because they knew how it felt to have real ones! "I wonder if we'll meet any of our fairy friends today," said Rachel. "Maybe they've already managed to find their magic objects."

She walked over to the nightstand and picked up *The Fairies' Book of Fairy Tales*. They had read it together last night, and the pink ribbon bookmark was still in the first story—*Sleeping Beauty.*

When Julia had got her magic jewelry box back, the first story had returned to the sparkly covered book. Kirsty peered over Rachel's shoulder as she turned to the second story, *Snow White*. But the pages were still blank.

"It looks as if Jack Frost still has the other six magic objects," said Kirsty, as Rachel flipped through the blank pages of the rest of the book.

"Then we just have to get them back before the Fairy Tale Festival is ruined," said Rachel in a determined voice. "But first we need to do each other's hair, right?"

"Right!" said Kirsty with a giggle.

They decorated each other's hair with glittery headbands, hair combs, and barrettes.

"The perfect finishing touch to our fairy outfits," said Rachel, looking at Kirsty with a smile. "Is there a mirror? I want to show you what I've done!"

She looked around and saw a hand
mirror lying on the nightstand. Carvings
of birds and butterflies decorated the
dark-wood frame and handle, and
the glass was old but beautifully polished.
Rachel held it up so that Kirsty could see
her reflection.

"How do
you think
I look?"
Kirsty
asked.

Rachel
opened
her mouth
to reply,
but before
she could

speak a silvery voice came from the mirror.

"Although you are pretty and ever so sweet, Snow White's the most beautiful princess you'll meet!"

Too Many Dwarves

The girls stared at the mirror in amazement.

"It's a talking mirror," said Kirsty. "I've never seen anything like it!"

"But you've read about it," said Rachel, suddenly excited. "We both have—in the story of *Snow White*!"

She turned the mirror around and looked into it. Her reflection gazed back at her. Feeling a little shy, Rachel cleared her throat.

"How do I look?" she asked.

At once, the silvery voice spoke again.

*"Although you're much fairer than many
    I've seen,
Snow White has more beauty than you or
    the queen."*

Rachel and Kirsty laughed and gazed into the mirror together.

"I'd love to see the real Snow White," said Kirsty. "She must be incredibly beautiful."

"She is," said a tinkling voice behind them.

"Look!" Rachel exclaimed.

In the mirror they could see the

reflection of a tiny fairy fluttering behind them.

"It's Eleanor the Snow White Fairy!" said Kirsty, whirling around. "Hello, Eleanor!"

Smiling, Eleanor flew over to land on the table. Her swishy lilac dress swirled out around her and her pretty dark hair was set off perfectly by her yellow headband.

"Good morning, Rachel and Kirsty," she said. "I see you've found the magic mirror."

"Is it really the one from the fairy tale?" Rachel asked.

"Yes, and I'm very glad to know where it is," said Eleanor, giving the mirror a little pat. "But all the characters are still lost, and the story will be ruined forever if I don't get back my magic jeweled hair comb."

"We'll help you to find Jack Frost and the goblins," Kirsty promised. "Hide in my backpack and we'll go downstairs and start searching."

Eleanor flew into Kirsty's backpack while Rachel tucked the magic mirror inside hers. Then they left their room at the top of the tower and hurried down the

winding stairs toward the main castle.
Halfway down, they saw a girl dressed
as Little Red Riding Hood.

"Hello!" called the
girls as they dashed
past her.

Little Red Riding Hood waved,
but Rachel and Kirsty had already
disappeared around the next bend. Next
they saw a boy dressed as Jack from *Jack
and the Beanstalk*.

"Morning!" called the girls as they
clattered down the remaining steps and
reached the hall.

The boy just stared after them with his
mouth open. Kirsty and Rachel giggled
as they ran past him.

"Why did he look so surprised?" asked Kirsty.

"Maybe he's never seen a fairy before," said Rachel, pointing at her wings with a laugh.

Just then, they heard loud noises of clattering, clanging, and shouting.

"It's coming from the castle kitchens!" Kirsty exclaimed. "Come on, let's go and find out what's wrong."

It didn't take them long to reach the kitchens. They burst through the doors and stared at the colorful scene in front of them. A beautiful young woman was trying to pack a picnic, surrounded by dwarves. They were juggling with boiled eggs, bowling with apples, and trying to balance sandwiches on their noses.

"Please, dwarves," said the young woman in a gentle voice. "You're really not helping—don't you *want* a nice picnic?"

"Yes—we want it right now!" said one of the dwarves.

He rammed some grapes into his mouth and chewed them with his mouth open.

"What bad manners!" Rachel exclaimed.

"They're not normally so rude to me," said the young woman, sounding upset. "We share a little cottage and they're usually very sweet."

"Oh my goodness," said Kirsty. "Are you Snow White?"

"Yes, how did you know?" Snow White asked.

"There's only one beautiful princess who shares a cottage with lots of dwarves," Kirsty replied, smiling. "But I thought there were only seven of them?"

"That's right," said Snow White, sounding surprised.

"But there are more than seven dwarves here," said Rachel. "Excuse me, everyone, would you all line up so that we can count you?"

After a lot of shoving, shuffling, and grumbling, the dwarves were standing in a very uneven line. Kirsty, Rachel, and Snow White walked along and counted them.

"Eleven," said Kirsty.

"There can't be!" said Snow White. "Let's count them again."

But halfway down the line, one of the

dwarves stuck out
his foot and Rachel
tripped over it. She
landed on her
knees and let
out a cry.

"Ha ha!
Did you have
a good trip?"
asked the dwarf.

Kirsty looked down and saw that
the dwarf who had tripped her up had
enormous feet. So did the dwarf next to
him—and the next two as well. They
were all snickering, and Kirsty recognized
the sneering sound very well.

"Those aren't dwarves!" she cried,
pulling Rachel to her feet. "They're
goblins!"

The Magic Comb

"RUN!" yelled the goblins.

They burst out through the kitchen door into the garden, and Kirsty ran after them, dragging Rachel behind her. They raced along gravel paths, past tall hedges and statues. Eleanor peeked out of Kirsty's backpack as they sprinted along.

"They're heading toward the forest!"
she cried. "You'll never catch them on
foot. Let me turn you into fairies—it'll
be quicker if we can all fly!"

Panting, the girls darted behind a high
hedge and Eleanor sprang out of the
backpack. She held up her wand and
waved it over Rachel and Kirsty. There
was a dazzling flash of silver
light, and when
the sparkles
cleared,
Rachel
and
Kirsty
were
hovering in
the air beside
Eleanor.

Their pretend wings had disappeared and been replaced by real gauzy fairy wings, and their fairy dresses were floating around them.

"The goblins have already gone into the forest," said Eleanor. "Come on—we can catch them if we hurry!"

Together, they zoomed into the forest and zipped through the trees, but there was no sign of the goblins. Eleanor swooped down and the girls followed her, looking for any sign that the goblins had passed that way. Then Rachel saw something on the ground.

"Look—a print!"
She pointed down at a large footprint in the mud.

"That's definitely a goblin footprint," said Kirsty, looking at the wide spaces between the toes. "Are there more? Maybe we could track them."

"Yes, over here!" called Eleanor, spotting another one.

The fairies flew on, following the trail of footprints through the muddiest part of the forest floor. After a few minutes, they heard voices—cackling, arguing voices.

"Those are goblins," said Rachel. "We must be close."

"I think there's a clearing up ahead," said Eleanor, who was in the lead. "Let's be careful."

They flew slowly and hid behind a bushy plant before peeking out into the clearing. Sure enough, the four goblins were there—still disguised as dwarves. They were standing beside a large pile of logs, looking upset and confused.

"Look—there's Jack Frost!" exclaimed
Kirsty.

The villain was sitting on a stool beside
a small pond. He was combing his hair
and beard, and admiring his reflection
in the water. As the fairies watched, he
half turned and glared
at the goblins.

"Why are
you all
standing
there like
lumps?"
he asked.
"Get on
with it!
I want a
cottage and I
want it NOW."

"But we've never built a cottage before," wailed the tallest of the goblins. "We don't know how!"

"That's not my problem," said Jack Frost. "I want it to look just like Snow White's cottage, only *better*. Stop being so lazy and start building!"

"Let's get closer," whispered Rachel.

She flew out of the plant and up to the leafy branches of a tree above the pond. Kirsty and Eleanor followed her, and they all looked down through the leaves at Jack Frost.

"I'm the prettiest in the land," Jack was saying to himself in a singsong voice. "There's no one as pretty as I am, not even Snow White!"

Suddenly, Eleanor gasped and almost fell off her branch. She had to flutter her wings to steady herself.

"What is it?" Kirsty asked in a low
voice.

"Look what he's using to comb his
hair," Eleanor whispered. "It's my magic
jeweled comb!"

The girls peered
down at the
delicate comb
in Jack Frost's
hand. It was
shaped like a
tiny silver bow,
and decorated
with shimmering
pearls.

"We've found it," said
Rachel with a relieved sigh. "Now
we just have to figure out a way to get
it back."

They all thought hard as Jack Frost continued to smile and nod at his watery reflection.

"There's no one as pretty as I am," he murmured. "Everyone is jealous of me, as they should be!"

"I've got an idea," said Kirsty. "He's more pleased with himself than anyone I've ever met. I think we could use that to help us get the comb back. Eleanor, could you turn me and Rachel into goblins?"

Eleanor nodded, and the three friends fluttered down to hide behind the tree. Rachel handed Eleanor the magic mirror, and then a swift flick of her fairy wand transformed Rachel and Kirsty into warty goblins. They couldn't help but giggle as they looked at each other. They looked so funny!

"Let's go," Kirsty said. "We have to convince Jack Frost to hand over the comb, and I think I know how!"

The Vainest of Them All

In their goblin disguises, Rachel and Kirsty stomped across the clearing toward Jack Frost. He scowled when he saw them.

"Go and help the others build my cottage," he demanded.

"But we just wanted to tell you something," said Kirsty quickly.

"Well?" Jack Frost snapped. "What is it?"

"Just that you are so handsome," said Kirsty. "Your hair is beautifully spiky and your beard is as icy and shiny as fresh snow."

Jack Frost couldn't help but smile proudly. He stroked his beard and puffed out his chest.

"I *am* magnificent," he agreed. "Carry on. More praise!"

"No one could look more wonderful than

you," said Rachel. "Oh please, may we have the honor of combing your beard for you?"

"No way," said Jack Frost, tightening his grip on the comb. "Goblins always tug too hard. You'll pull my hair out by the roots!"

"We'll be careful," Kirsty promised.

But Jack Frost shook his head.

"I can comb it better myself," he said. "You two can't make it look pretty enough."

Rachel and Kirsty exchanged worried looks. Then a different idea popped into Rachel's head.

"I know where's there's a wonderful mirror," she said in a boastful voice. "You could see yourself much better than in the pond reflection. I could get it for you—if you'd let me have the comb as a reward."

"I want that mirror, but I'm not giving you the comb," Jack Frost said. "Get me the mirror! Don't be so greedy!"

Rachel and Kirsty didn't dare to argue with him anymore.

They backed away, and Jack Frost
returned to gazing at his own reflection.
The girls hurried behind the tree in their
goblin disguises, and found Eleanor
waiting for them.

"I'm sorry," said Kirsty with a frown.
"I really thought my
idea would work."

"It's OK," said
Eleanor. "It was
a good try.
We'll just have
to think of
something
else."

They all stared
at each other,
but they couldn't
think of a single plan.

Then they heard the sound of branches cracking and plants being crushed underfoot. A shrill voice was shouting something, and they all listened hard as the noise grew louder. Someone was crashing through the forest toward the clearing, and they sounded very angry. After a few seconds, the fairies were able to make out the words.

"Where's my magic mirror?" the high-pitched voice was shouting. "Give me my magic mirror!"

The voice sent shivers down the girls' backs.

"Who could it be?" asked Kirsty in a whisper.

"It's the wicked queen," said Eleanor. "She's Snow White's stepmother, and she's obsessed with staring into the mirror

because she's so terribly vain. She always asks it the same question."

"She wants to know 'Who is the prettiest of them all?' doesn't she?" asked Rachel, remembering the story. "And one day the mirror starts saying 'Snow White,' and the wicked queen is furious."

Eleanor nodded, and Kirsty gave a little cry of excitement.

"I know!" she said. "Eleanor, can you use your magic to make the mirror say Jack Frost's name?"

"Yes, I think so," said Eleanor. "But how will that help?"

"Because if *we* can't make Jack Frost give up the mirror, maybe the wicked queen can," Kirsty explained. "She sounds pretty scary!"

Eleanor waved her wand over the mirror and spoke the words of a spell.

"We need to save my magic comb.
Please help us and you'll soon be home.
Instead of talking about Snow White,
Name Jack Frost as the prettiest sight."

The mirror sparkled, and the three fairies looked at each other.

"Now we have to get Jack Frost to look into it," said Kirsty.

"That should be easy," said Rachel, standing up. "There's nothing he likes better than looking at himself."

"Bring me my magic mirror!" yelled the voice of the wicked queen.

She was very close now, and it seemed to the girls that even the leaves were shaking at the sound of her voice.

"Hurry, Rachel!" cried Eleanor. "She's almost here!"

The Prettiest in the Land

Just as the wicked queen pushed through the trees into the clearing, Rachel ran over to Jack Frost and held the mirror in front of his face. He gave an admiring "oooh" of delight and started to comb his beard again.

"I'm so pretty!" he said, giving himself a loving smile.

At once, the silvery voice of the mirror spoke to him.

"Oh, fair Jack Frost, indeed it's true.
The prettiest in all the land is YOU!"

When he heard this, Jack Frost leaped to his feet and happily ran around the pond.

"I'm the prettiest and the best!" he shouted. "I'm the prettiest and the—oh."

He spotted the wicked queen's shadow and stopped in his tracks. He looked slowly up at her face, and then his knees began to knock together.

Kirsty ran across to join Rachel, leaving Eleanor hovering beside the tree.

"She looks really scary," Kirsty whispered into Rachel's ear.

Clearly Jack Frost thought so, too. He shook as the queen glared at him. She was dressed in a swirling black cloak and wore a spiky silver crown. Her dark hair was streaked with white strands, and there were tiny lines around her eyes, but she was very beautiful. Then her mouth twisted into a snarl, and she didn't look beautiful anymore.

"You're not the prettiest in the land!"
she screeched. "It's me! Me, me, ME!"

She picked up her cloak and lunged
toward Jack Frost, who yelled in fear and
threw his hands into the air. The magic
jeweled comb flew up and then fell
toward the middle of the pond.

"I can't reach it!" cried Rachel as the comb went over their heads.

"But I can!" Eleanor called out, swooping away from the tree toward the pond.

With her hands outstretched, she managed to catch the comb just before it hit the water. It shrank to fairy size at once and Eleanor flew up, laughing with joy.

"My comb!" she exclaimed. "At last I can take it back where it belongs!"

Jack Frost was too busy apologizing to the wicked queen to pay any attention to Eleanor.

"I'm sorry!" he whimpered. "You're right! Whatever you say—whatever you want—you're right!"

Eleanor fluttered down beside Rachel and Kirsty. A single touch of her wand transformed them into humans again, and they were once more wearing their fairy outfits and backpacks.

"My magic comb is safe, thanks to

you," Eleanor said. "It's time to return all things to their rightful owners."

She looked at the mirror, and then at the wicked queen.

"Of course," said Rachel, thinking of the Snow White fairy tale. "I had forgotten that the mirror belongs to the queen."

She walked slowly toward the angry queen, who was towering over Jack Frost.

"I'm right beside you," said Kirsty, slipping her hand into Rachel's hand.

"Excuse me?" Rachel asked the queen, feeling very nervous. "I think this belongs to you."

The queen turned her flashing eyes on Rachel, who held out the mirror. The queen snatched it, held it up, and gazed at her reflection.

"Tell me the truth once and for all!"
she shrieked. "Who is the prettiest in
all the land?"

For a moment, everyone in the clearing
held their breaths.

1

"Snow White, of course," the mirror replied.

The wicked queen let out a squeal of rage . . . and then shimmered and faded back to her fairy tale.

A Fairy Tale Picnic

As the queen disappeared, the girls heard happy voices echoing from among the trees. Then the bushes parted and Snow White stepped into the clearing, followed by the seven dwarves. They were carrying a large picnic hamper, plates, and drinks. Snow White skipped happily when she saw Rachel and Kirsty.

"Thank you for your help!" she called to them, as the dwarves put the hamper down. "Enjoy the picnic!"

The girls waved to her and then she and the dwarves shimmered and disappeared.

"They've returned to their fairy tale," said Eleanor, landing on Kirsty's shoulder. "Thanks to you both, Snow White and all the other characters are back where they belong."

"That's wonderful," said Kirsty. "Another happy ending."

"Not for everyone," said Rachel, looking across at Jack Frost.

He had slumped down on his stool and rested his chin in his hands. The goblins abandoned their half-built log cottage and gathered around him.

"Don't be sad," said the shortest goblin.

"You can yell at me if you want," said another goblin.

Jack Frost lifted his head and peered at his sad reflection in the pond. His bottom lip wobbled.

"I *am* the prettiest in the land," he muttered.

"You *are*!" shouted the goblins. "Of course you are! That Snow White can't compete with you."

"She didn't even have a beard," added the tallest goblin.

Jack Frost started to look a little happier, and the girls grinned at each other.

"I think it's time for us to go back to the castle," said Rachel.

"And for me to return to Fairyland," said Eleanor. "Thank you for everything! I can't wait to tell the other fairies that another of our fairy tales is safe again!"

With a happy wave of her hand, she vanished back to Fairyland. Rachel and Kirsty looked down at the picnic hamper.

"Let's take this back with us," Kirsty suggested.

Together, they lifted the heavy basket and carried it back through the forest, along the gravel paths and past the tall hedges and statues. By the time they reached the castle, they were feeling very hungry indeed. They saw a group of children sitting on the grass and waved. The children dressed as Little Red Riding Hood and Jack from *Jack and the Beanstalk* waved back at them.

"Look, there are the girl and boy we saw earlier," said Rachel. "I wonder if they'd like to share the picnic with us."

They went over to ask them, and the children agreed happily. A short time later, everyone was sitting on a large picnic blanket in the middle of the largest lawn. Rachel and Kirsty had quickly made a lot of new friends. Little Red Riding Hood's name was Emily, and

the boy dressed as Jack was named Aaron. Everyone had enjoyed Snow White's wonderful picnic, and they were all full and happy.

"Maybe someone should tell a story," said Emily in a sleepy voice.

"We've got the perfect book upstairs," said Rachel, jumping to her feet. "I'll go and get it."

She ran into the castle and up the winding staircase to the tower bedroom. A few moments later she hurried back across the lawn and sat down with the other children.

"That was quick," said Kirsty.

"I ran all the way," Rachel panted, handing her the sparkling *The Fairies' Book of Fairy Tales*. "You read it, Kirsty— I'm all out of breath."

Kirsty opened the book and turned to the second story. The words and pictures had returned, and she held up the pages to show Rachel. The girls shared a secret smile and then Kirsty started to read.

"Once upon a time there was a young princess named Snow White . . ."

Rachel turned the pages, and everyone listened, enchanted, as Kirsty read the story. When she finished, everyone clapped, but Rachel turned the next page and sighed. The following pages were still blank, and the girls exchanged a worried look.

"Five fairy tales are still missing," said Rachel in a low voice.

"And there are five more magic objects to find," Kirsty added. "Oh, Rachel, I wonder what our next fairy tale adventure will be!"

THE FAIRY TALE FAIRIES

Rachel and Kirsty found
Julia's and Eleanor's missing magic objects.
Now it's time for them to help

Faith
the Cinderella Fairy!

Join their next adventure in this
special sneak peek . . .

A Tiptop Morning

"Another beautiful day at Tiptop Castle!" exclaimed Rachel Walker, throwing open the window and breathing in the crisp morning air.

She was looking out of the bedroom that she was sharing with her best friend, Kirsty Tate. They had been having a fun

time at the Fairy Tale Festival, and
they couldn't wait for this morning's
ballroom-dancing lesson.

"I can't believe how lucky we are,"
said Kirsty, who was brushing her hair at
the beautiful vanity table. "It's amazing
that the festival is being held here, so
close to Tippington—and we've made
some great new friends."

"We should go down to the ballroom,"
said Kirsty, looking at her alarm clock.
"The ballroom-dancing lesson will be
starting soon and I don't want to miss a
second!"

The girls hurried down the spiral
staircase, still thinking about their fairy
friends. So far, they had helped Julia the
Sleeping Beauty Fairy and Eleanor
the Snow White Fairy get their magic

objects back. Now Sleeping Beauty and her prince and Snow White and the seven dwarves were all back inside their worlds. But there were still five magic objects left to find, and many more fairy tale characters to return to their stories.

RAINBOW magic™

Which Magical Fairies Have You Met?

- ❏ The Rainbow Fairies
- ❏ The Weather Fairies
- ❏ The Jewel Fairies
- ❏ The Pet Fairies
- ❏ The Dance Fairies
- ❏ The Music Fairies
- ❏ The Sports Fairies
- ❏ The Party Fairies
- ❏ The Ocean Fairies
- ❏ The Night Fairies
- ❏ The Magical Animal Fairies
- ❏ The Princess Fairies
- ❏ The Superstar Fairies
- ❏ The Fashion Fairies
- ❏ The Sugar & Spice Fairies
- ❏ The Earth Fairies
- ❏ The Magical Crafts Fairies
- ❏ The Baby Animal Rescue Fairies
- ❏ The Fairy Tale Fairies

■ SCHOLASTIC

Find all of your favorite fairy friends at
scholastic.com/rainbowmagic

RMFAIRY13

RAINBOW magic™

Magical fun for everyone!
Learn fairy secrets, send friendship notes, and more!

HIT entertainment

www.scholastic.com/rainbowmagic

RMACTIV4

RAINBOW magic™
SPECIAL EDITION

Which Magical Fairies Have You Met?

- ❏ Joy the Summer Vacation Fairy
- ❏ Holly the Christmas Fairy
- ❏ Kylie the Carnival Fairy
- ❏ Stella the Star Fairy
- ❏ Shannon the Ocean Fairy
- ❏ Trixie the Halloween Fairy
- ❏ Gabriella the Snow Kingdom Fairy
- ❏ Juliet the Valentine Fairy
- ❏ Mia the Bridesmaid Fairy
- ❏ Flora the Dress-Up Fairy
- ❏ Paige the Christmas Play Fairy
- ❏ Emma the Easter Fairy
- ❏ Cara the Camp Fairy
- ❏ Destiny the Rock Star Fairy
- ❏ Belle the Birthday Fairy

- ❏ Olympia the Games Fairy
- ❏ Selena the Sleepover Fairy
- ❏ Cheryl the Christmas Tree Fairy
- ❏ Florence the Friendship Fairy
- ❏ Lindsay the Luck Fairy
- ❏ Brianna the Tooth Fairy
- ❏ Autumn the Falling Leaves Fairy
- ❏ Keira the Movie Star Fairy
- ❏ Addison the April Fool's Day Fairy
- ❏ Bailey the Babysitter Fairy
- ❏ Natalie the Christmas Stocking Fairy
- ❏ Lila and Myla the Twins Fairies
- ❏ Chelsea the Congratulations Fairy
- ❏ Carly the School Fairy
- ❏ Angelica the Angel Fairy
- ❏ Blossom the Flower Girl Fairy

3 stories in each one!

SCHOLASTIC
Find all of your favorite fairy friends at
scholastic.com/rainbowmagic

HIT entertainment

RMSPECIAL17